fred and fiona

fuzzy blue monsters with finicky fur

[signatures]

written by
renu, natasha, and
serena Mansukhani

illustrated by david kcenich

Archway Publishing books may be ordered through booksellers or by contacting:

Archway Publishing
1663 Liberty Drive
Bloomington, IN 47403
www.archwaypublishing.com
1 (888) 242-5904

Because of the dynamic nature of the Internet, any web addresses or links contained in this book may have changed since publication and may no longer be valid. The views expressed in this work are solely those of the author and do not necessarily reflect the views of the publisher, and the publisher hereby disclaims any responsibility for them.

ISBN: 978-1-4808-3159-9 (sc)
ISBN: 978-1-4808-3160-5 (e)

Print information available on the last page.

Archway Publishing rev. date: 08/15/2016

FOR DADDY, NANA, OTHER GROWN-UPS,
KIDS, AND STUFFED ANIMALS EVERYWHERE,
WHO LIKE TO CAUSE A LITTLE TROUBLE.
SPECIAL THANKS TO MICHELLE O'BRIEN

Fred and Fiona were twins. They were eight years old. Actually, at any one time, Fiona was always a few minutes older than Fred, because she was born first.

But the most important thing about Fred and Fiona was that they were fuzzy, funny, and trouble-causing blue monsters with LOTS of finicky fur.

They lived in a house with Mommy Monster and Daddy Monster, and they each had their own room. Boy, did they love their rooms!

Fred and Fiona's rooms were next to each other, with a window built into the wall between so they could see each other and talk to each other if they felt like it.

Each one had a blue letter "F" hanging on the wall over their bed.

Fiona's "F" had a pink bow on it that exactly matched the pink bow she always wore in her fur.

The only thing Fred and Fiona didn't like about their rooms was cleaning them up.

One day, mommy called upstairs and said it was time to clean up.

"But mooooomeeeeee," said Fred, "Can't we clean our rooms tomorrow?"

"Sorry," said mommy, "They are too messy."

"Aw, man!" Fred and Fiona chimed in unison.

Fred and Fiona had a good reason to put off cleaning their rooms; they looked as if a big thunderstorm had blown through and scattered everything about.

And today was a cleaner day than usual!

After a while, when mommy asked them to clean their rooms for the third time, they finally got started.

There was one thing Fred and Fiona actually did like about cleaning: VACUUMING.

Their carpet used to be white, but lately it had been looking more bluish in color, and they could not figure out why.

Fred started vacuuming first. As he was vacuuming, he noticed that the vacuum wasn't really sucking up anything. It seemed to be spitting out more stuff on the carpet than it was picking up.

"That's odd," he said. "The vacuum isn't working!"

"Let me see it," said Fiona, as she took the vacuum from Fred. At first, she couldn't figure out what was wrong either.

Then, she pushed the button that opened the vacuum canister.

SUDDENLY, a HUGE big blue ball of monster fur popped out of the vacuum!!

Fred and Fiona stood there with their mouths open.

"Oh my oranges!" exclaimed Fred, "There's a monster living in our vacuum!"

"That is NOT a monster living in our vacuum!" said Fiona, "That is our FUR!"

"WOW..." said Fred, "That's a LOT of fur we have been shedding."

"We are fuzzy monsters; we shed, what can we do?" said Fiona. "We should go tell mommy so she can throw this out."

Suddenly, Fred had an idea. He took a deep breath.

"Wait Fiona, let's keep it!"

"You want to keep it? Why??"

"Look at it!" whispered Fred, "It's awesome!"

He went and stood next to the fur ball. "Look," said Fred, "The monster fur ball looks exactly like me!"

Fiona realized he had a point. The fur ball had a real resemblance to Fred; it was about the same size and shape as he was.

"See Fiona? I could pretend the fur ball is me, like when mommy says to brush my teeth, I could just put it in the bathroom, and she will walk by and think I am doing what she asked!"

"I don't know if that's a good idea, Fred..."

"I'm going to try it!" said Fred.

Just then mommy called, "Hey kids, it's time to brush your teeth before bed!"

"OK, mommy!"

Fred went into the bathroom and put the ball of fur in front of the sink where he normally stood. He then stuck his toothbrush into the ball of fur where his mouth would be. He closed the door but left it open just a little bit. He then snuck back into his bedroom.

They heard mommy coming upstairs. "Fred! I thought I told you to brush your teeth!"

"I am!" called Fred from his room.

Mommy peeked into the bathroom. "Oh yes, I see you are, Fred. Good job!"

She went back downstairs.

Fiona stood there astonished as Fred smiled.

"No way!" she squealed. "It worked! I want to try! I want to try!"

So she took one of her pink bows and stuck it in the ball of fur.

"I am going to try something in the morning." She hid the ball of fur in her closet overnight.

Fiona did not like to get up in the morning. She just was not a morning monster.

So the next day, when mommy called, "Wake up you two! It's time for school!" Fiona said sleepily from her bed, "All right...I'm getting up."

She got the fur ball out of her closet and put it at the top of the stairs, so mommy would see it and think she was up. Then she went back to bed.

"Oh good, Fiona" said mommy, looking up, "I see you're up!"

"Fred," said Fiona from her bed, "This fur ball is the best thing ever!"

"See, I told you!" said Fred giggling. He went downstairs.

Meanwhile, Fiona fell back asleep. After a while, mommy was getting impatient that Fiona had not come down.

She called, "Fiona Monster, you come downstairs right now!"

All you could hear from Fiona were snoring noises.

Mommy walked upstairs, saw the ball of fur, and realized it wasn't Fiona!

"Oh my apples! Where did this come from?! What is it doing here?!"

Fiona woke up, jumped out of bed, and ran to the hall. "Well mommy..., remember when we were vacuuming yesterday?" she began.

"See, the vacuum wasn't working, and we opened it, and...," said Fred, looking at the fur ball.

"We're sorry," they said together, looking at the floor.

Mommy now understood what Fiona had done and that Fred had tricked her last night as well.

"I cannot believe you both tried to trick me this way and pretend that ball of fur was you!"

She started chuckling a little. "Though it is kind of ingenious."

Later that day, after Fred and Fiona's room was finally fur-less, the ball of fur was in the garbage can outside.

Daddy came home from work, saw it, and came running inside.

"Oh my lemons, Oh my lemons!"

Mommy came running into the room, "What? What?!"

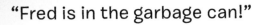

"Fred is in the garbage can!"

"Oh that. That's not Fred, it's the ball of fur."

"What?! What are you talking about?"

And they told him the whole story.

THE END

About the Authors and Illustrator

Renu Mansukhani, and her daughters, Natasha and Serena, live in Arlington, Virginia. They invented Fred and Fiona and made up stories about them a few years ago when Renu, a working mom, was falling asleep while reading bedtime stories, as a way to keep her awake. They taped a story on her phone each night. Eventually, they realized other kids might enjoy hearing about Fred and Fiona's adventures as well, and decided it would be a great project for them all to publish one of their stories about these cute characters. After some hard work, help of friends and family, and luck in finding David, they are thrilled with the result.

David Kcenich is a cartoonist and former Disney animator who has ventured into the children's book world of illustration. He lives in California and spends most of his time drawing and chasing his own fuzzy blue monster, Caroline, around the house. He was thrilled to be asked to illustrate this book and looks forward to bringing you more of Fred and Fiona's adventures in the future.

CPSIA information can be obtained
at www.ICGtesting.com
Printed in the USA
BVOW07s2321260916

463392BV00003B/4/P